D0595737

Design and Art Direction by Michaelis/Carpelis Design Assoc.
Cover illustration by Mathew Archambault.
Interior illustrations by Frank Mayo.

Copyright © 1995 Steck-Vaughn Company.
All rights reserved. Published by Scholastic Inc., 557 Broadway,
New York, NY 10012, by arrangement with Steck-Vaughn Company.
Printed in the U.S.A.

ISBN 0-439-12365-8
(meets NASTA specifications)

6 7 8 9 10   23   10 09 08 07 06

DANGEROUS GAME

by Traccy West

4230500020033408

SCHOLASTIC INC.

New York Toronto London Auckland Sydney
Mexico City New Delhi Hong Kong Buenos Aires

Chapter · 1

"Give it up, Sean! You'll never tag me now!"

Sean Albertie stopped running and looked in the direction of the teasing voice. Tom Perez stood high above him on the pedestrian bridge that crossed the highway.

"Don't be so sure, Tom!" Sean yelled back. He headed down the footpath toward the long flight of stairs leading up to the bridge.

Sean started to feel the strain as he neared the end of the steps. He was in good shape, but he had been chasing Tom Perez on foot for an hour now.

It was dark on the bridge, since only a few of the spotlights were working. Sean couldn't see Tom up ahead.

"That was careless of Tom to draw attention to himself like that," Sean thought. "He probably figured he had the advantage." Sean glanced at the glowing numbers of his digital sports watch. 9:56 p.m. He only had four minutes to tag Tom.

Sean patted the tin box of paint pellets in his pocket.

Sean reached the other end of the bridge and headed down the stairs. He was out of breath. Tom sure knew what he was doing. The stairs led into the crowded parking lot of Funworld Amusement Park. The park closed at 11 p.m., but people were already pouring into the parking lot. Spotting Tom here would be like finding a needle in a haystack.

Sean leaned back against a parked car

and caught his breath. He couldn't lose this game—not when he was so close.

Three months ago, when Sean first transferred to East City High, he would never have guessed that this was how he'd be spending his Saturday nights.

It all sort of happened by accident. On his first day at school, some of the guys from Sean's homeroom had approached him.

"Hey, do you play Quarry?" one of them had asked.

Sean had shrugged. "Sure." He didn't want to seem like a jerk.

"Cool. Then be at the diner at 6:30 on Saturday night."

Sean wasn't sure what to expect. Quarry sounded like some kind of board game.

He was surprised to find out that the "quarry" was a living, breathing person. Each week, a different kid from the Quarry Society was chosen as "it." The quarry would have a thirty-minute head start to disappear into the city. The other kids would follow clues the quarry left along the trail. They'd have three hours to find and tag the quarry with a paint pellet. Each society member had his or her own special color.

Sean was good at figuring out the clues, and he was in good shape from being on the track team at his old school. In just a few weeks, he had become one of the top members of the

Quarry Society. Sean and another player, Rita Davenport, were now tied for the highest number of quarry tags.

"Funworld closes in one hour!" boomed a voice over the loudspeakers.

Sean tensed up. "I've got to concentrate," he thought. "Tom can't be far away."

Sean ran down the nearest aisle of cars, scanning the crowd ahead of him.

Where was Tom?

Quickly, Sean realized his mistake. Tom would take advantage of the natural cover the cars provided. Crouching down, Sean kept his eyes low to the ground.

Bingo! On the other side of a red sports car, Sean spotted Tom's trademark white high-tops. Sean pulled a tin box out of his pocket. Then he quickly flipped open the lid and palmed a red paint pellet.

"Game's over, Tom!" Sean yelled as he ran around the car. There was no time to aim carefully. Sean pitched the paint pellet in Tom's direction.

Sean watched his red waterpaint pellet explode on Tom's arm as if in slow motion. At the same time, a streak of yellow came whizzing from the other direction.

"I almost made it!" Tom said, shaking his head. "You got me, man!"

Just then, a figure stepped out of the
darkness. It was Rita Davenport.

"No way, Sean," Rita said. "This tag is
mine!"

Chapter · 2

"What do you mean, your tag?" Sean fumed. "I got him first. Here's proof." He pointed to the red paint splotch on Tom's arm.

Rita's dark eyes were flashing. She grabbed Sean by the arm and pulled him around to Tom's back. "That's yellow paint. That's my tag."

Sean turned to Tom. "I tagged you first, Tom. Tell her."

Tom shrugged. "I'm not sure which one of you guys tagged me first. It all happened so fast. I guess you guys are still tied."

Rita looked like she was going to

explode. "Oh no you don't! I won't stand being tied with this amateur for another minute."

"Well, don't think I'm too crazy about it, either," Sean said.

Tom stepped between them. "Calm down, you two. I'm the one who should be complaining. Look what you did to my new shirt." He pointed to the red and yellow paint splotches.

Rita rolled her eyes. "Oh, boo hoo.

You know this stuff is waterpaint and it washes off easily. If you hadn't been worried about your shirt, maybe you would have seen the truth—that I hit you first."

Sean shook his head. "It's not Tom's fault, Rita. Let's settle this at the diner. The rest of the Quarry Society should be there soon. "

Rita glared at him. "This isn't over." She jogged off and disappeared into the

Funworld parking lot.

"She's got a lot of nerve," Sean said.

"Lighten up, man," Tom said. "It's just a game. Rita will calm down while she's driving herself over to the diner. By the way, where's your car?"

"I ditched it downtown when I started chasing you on foot," Sean said. "We have to walk back."

Five minutes later, the boys reached Sean's car, a beat-up compact that used to belong to his dad. It wasn't much, but it got him around. Most of the Quarry Society members had gotten their driver's licenses in the last few months. Wheels moved the game to a whole new level.

"Man, I just don't get Rita sometimes," Sean told Tom as they drove to the diner. "I mean, in school she's okay. But when we play Quarry, it's like she's a different person. All she cares about is winning, no matter what she has to do."

"It's a matter of pride," Tom said. "Rita founded the Quarry Society over a year ago. She was always the best player. You only started a few months ago, and you've already tied her record. That's got to sting."

"I guess you're right," Sean said. "It's just that sometimes it feels like she thinks she can get anything she wants because her dad's so rich."

Tom shook his head. "That's not really true. Give Rita a chance, Sean. She's not so bad. Besides, you were acting pretty competitive yourself tonight."

Sean didn't answer. He knew Tom was probably right.

"Ah, The Wild Western Diner," Tom said as they pulled into the parking lot. "My home away from home."

The diner was a popular hangout for high school kids. At this hour, it was packed. Sean and Tom spotted Rita and the other members of the Quarry Society at their regular booth.

"Well, look who it is," Rita said. She was smiling, but Sean could hear the irritation in her voice.

A junior named Brian Markinson punched Tom playfully on the arm. "Tough break, man. I heard it was really close."

Rita's eyes narrowed. "Too close."

"I'll try to be cool," Sean promised

himself quietly. He studied Rita.

She had long dark hair and always dressed simply when she was chasing quarry. Sean kept his own blond hair cut short. It made things easier, no hair falling in the eyes. He even thought about getting a crew cut when summer started.

Sean slid into the booth across from Rita. For the first time, he noticed an unusual silver object on a chain around her neck. It was a crescent moon.

"Hey, that's pretty cool," Sean remarked. "Does it mean anything special?"

Rita fingered the chain necklace. She smiled, and Sean thought for a second that she looked really friendly. "Thanks. It's a symbol of the Roman goddess Diana, who ruled the hunt. I wear it for luck during Quarry."

"I guess it's not all that lucky," Kara Silwitz, another society member, joked.

Rita's smile vanished, and she looked annoyed again. "I have a way to settle this tie once and for all," she said, raising her voice. "That is, if Sean here is up to the challenge."

Sean stiffened. "I'm up for anything you can come up with. Just name it."

The table got quiet. Rita leaned over the table toward Sean. "Okay, hotshot. These are my terms," she said. "We have a one-on-one match next Saturday at sundown, just you and me. The winner becomes head of the Quarry Society. The loser has to quit the society for good."

A murmur went through the society members. "That's pretty harsh, Rita," Brian said. "Come on, don't make him agree to that."

"It's no problem. I won't be the one quitting," Sean said. "I just have one question: who tags, and who's quarry?"

"We'll flip a coin," Rita said.

"Fair enough," Sean said. "Who's got a quarter?"

Tom held up a silver coin.

"Just to show you I'm a good sport, you call it," Rita said.

"If it's tails, I tag. If it's heads, you tag," Sean said.

"That's fair," Rita said. "Flip it, Tom."

Tom threw the coin in the air and slapped it against the back of his hand

as it came down. "Tails!" he announced. "Sean tags, Rita's quarry."

Rita slid out of the booth. "Then it's settled. Expect your first clue at sundown next Saturday." She walked toward the door, then turned around. "Good luck, Sean. You're going to need lots of it!"

Chapter · 3

The following Saturday, Sean watched the last rays of the sunset from his bedroom window. He wore a dark T-shirt and a pair of black jeans. It was just as important to blend into the background when you were tagging as when you were quarry.

Sean checked his equipment one last time. He had put an extra supply of paint pellets in his flip-top box. He switched his flashlight off and on a few times. He was all set.

Sean walked into the kitchen, grabbed his car keys, and left a brief note for his parents. He was feeling pretty excited about tonight's game. It was a good kind of nervousness, Sean thought. It was the kind that makes you sharp and alert.

Sean stepped into the warm night air and looked around. Rita had said to expect his first clue at sundown. Sean figured she would find some way of getting it to him.

He was right. Taped to his car's windshield was a note. Rita knew what

she was doing, he had to admit. He'd been keeping an eye on his car all afternoon.

Sean unfolded the note and read it. "Where I'm going, people are dying to get in. The view is great." Rita had drawn a small crescent moon at the bottom of the page.

Sean laughed smugly. The clue was an easy one—dying to get in, nice view, the crescent moon. They all pointed to one place: the Crestview Cemetery. Rita had given such an easy clue on purpose. She knew that cemeteries spooked Sean. She was trying to psyche him out.

"I can't let that happen," Sean told himself. He jumped into his car and gunned the engine. There was no time to waste.

Crestview Cemetery was about fifteen minutes from Sean's house. It was inside city limits, so it was acceptable Quarry territory. But knowing Rita she would make him waste his precious time driving all over the city.

By the time Sean pulled up in front of the cemetery gates there was no trace of the sun in the sky. The street was lit, but inside the cemetery it was eerily dark.

Sean climbed out of his car and took a deep breath. "I've got to go through with this," he thought. "With any luck, I'll tag her right here, and this whole thing will be over."

The cemetery gate was unlocked, and it creaked loudly when Sean pushed it open. Stepping inside, Sean could hear nothing except for an occasional cricket chirping.

"What now?" Sean wondered. But a rustling sound ahead answered his question. Sean thought he heard faint laughter.

"May as well go that way," Sean mused. He headed in the direction of the laughter.

Marble gravestones loomed out of the ground like crooked teeth. Was Rita hiding behind one of them? No, that would be too easy.

Sean clicked on his flashlight. There was no way he was going to find Rita in the dark. The faint laughter rang again a few feet ahead, and Sean nearly

jumped out of his skin.

The light from the flashlight revealed a small wooden shed. A crescent moon was carved above the door.

"That's got to be it," Sean whispered to himself.

Sean approached the shed slowly. It was probably some kind of tool shed. Was Rita inside? "Maybe I should try climbing through a window," Sean thought.

He quickly scrapped that idea when he saw that the windows were at least eight feet above the ground.

Sean reached for his pellet box with his free hand. He flipped out a red pellet. Now there was nothing to do but go through the front door. If Rita was in there, he'd be ready for her.

Sean slowly pushed the door inward. From the corner of his eye, he thought he saw a piece of rope attached to the doorknob, but his mind didn't really register it. He had to know if Rita was inside. He pushed the door open just wide enough to sneak in.

The shed was empty except for a rusty water pump. Sean's first instinct was to breathe a sigh of relief. Then he noticed a closet built into the shed's back wall. There was another crescent moon on its door, but this one looked as if it had been freshly painted.

"Rita?" Sean whispered softly. He

stepped to the side of the closet and slowly opened the door. A lifeless, dark-haired figure lurched out and crashed to the floor.

Sean stifled a scream. His heart was pounding. He found his voice again. "Rita?"

He bent down to get a closer look. It was a cloth dummy! Sean turned the figure over onto its back. Rita's painted face stared up at him with an evil grin. The dummy's hands had fallen over its chest like a corpse. Sean groaned, half in relief. Then he pulled a note from between the dummy's fingers.

"I'd like to see you break this tic, Sean," the note read. "If you can't, maybe you should just give up and do some shopping instead."

Bang! The loud slam of the shed door rocked the small room. Sean leapt to his feet and ran to the door. It wouldn't budge.

"How could I be so stupid?" Sean kicked the door in anger. He paced around the room for a few seconds, then stopped. "I've got to keep my cool.

I've just got to figure a way to get out of here," Sean said out loud.

Sean glanced up, remembering the window he had seen earlier. It would be a tight squeeze. Luckily, the water pump stood right underneath the window. Sean used the pump to boost himself up to the tiny opening. He climbed through and fell to the ground outside with a crash.

Sean steadied himself and ran around

to the front of the shed. He hoped to find Rita still there, enjoying her joke. Sean saw that Rita had tied the door closed by attaching a thick piece of rope to a nearby tree.

Sean heard a crashing through the brush, then Rita's footsteps running across the cemetery, away from the gates. "She must have her car parked on the next block," Sean thought. "That note probably means she's headed to the Galleria shopping mall."

Sean considered running after her, but decided against it. Rita had a head start, and she was a good runner. He'd have a better chance beating her to the mall in his car.

"You may have won this round, Rita," Sean thought, "but this game is definitely not over!"

Chapter · 4

Tires squealed as Rita's car turned the corner three blocks up ahead. Sean kept his foot on the gas pedal. He could feel it. The end of this game was coming up!

Suddenly, a blue sports car pulled out of the gas station across the street and cut Sean off. The car zoomed ahead and caught up to Rita's white convertible.

Sean was puzzled. What was going on? Rita was still playing games with him, Sean guessed. He pounded on the steering wheel angrily. Rita putting that other car between them just wasn't playing fair.

Sean weighed his options. The

Eastern Highway was up ahead. That was the quickest way to the Galleria from here, and Sean knew Rita would take it. If he could keep her in sight until they got to the highway, he could try pulling up next to her and tagging her in her car. She had the convertible top down. With any luck, both of them would have to stop for the red light at

the same time. Then it would be a piece of cake. And Sean would be the Quarry champ!

Sean managed to keep Rita in sight. Soon, a large intersection loomed up ahead. The highway was three lanes wide, and Sean could see Rita in the second lane from the right. The blue sports car stayed right behind her.

Picking up speed, Sean edged into the third lane from the right. "Please turn red," he willed the light. "Yes!" The light was changing, and Rita was slowing down. The light turned red. Rita was a sitting duck.

Sean pulled up alongside the convertible and stopped. He kept his left hand on the steering wheel and reached for a paint pellet with his right. Sean looked right and grinned. Rita turned and looked back at him, fury written on her face. Sean aimed as best as he could and tossed the paint pellet. But at the same time Rita quickly swung her car to the right, into the first lane. The red paint splattered harmlessly on her rear bumper.

When the light changed, Sean tried to get over into the right lane, right behind Rita, but the blue car cut him off and followed Rita into the first lane.

"Jerks!" Sean screamed. The driver of the blue car, an older man, shot Sean a dirty look. Then the light turned green. Sean watched helplessly as Rita and the blue car made the right off of the highway, a stream of traffic following them. There was no way he could make the turn and follow them. Already, cars behind him were honking angrily.

"All right, all right," Sean muttered, stepping on the gas.

Traffic stretched out far ahead of him. Rita probably knew some shortcut to the mall, Sean figured. After all, she had been living in this city a lot longer than he had lived here.

He gritted his teeth and looked at his watch again. Time was passing quickly.

Over half of Sean's time was up already. Until now, the thought of having to quit the Quarry Society hadn't seemed real. But the way Rita was playing tonight, he had to face facts. He might lose.

"I don't need dirty tricks to win this thing," Sean muttered. "I'll just have to catch Rita at the Galleria."

Fifteen minutes later, Sean pulled into the mall's parking lot. There was no sign of Rita's convertible or the blue car.

"That's all right. At least I've figured out what I've got to look for," Sean said to himself. "I've just got to keep my eyes open for crescent moons."

But where would he find a crescent moon in the mall? Shoppers stared as Sean, covered with dirt from his climb

through the shed window, ran past them checking out the stores.

There was no sign of Rita in Captain Midnight's Record Shack. She wasn't in the Galaxy Telescope Shop, either. Sean even tried the croissant stand in the food court. After all, croissant rolls were shaped like crescent moons. But that proved useless, too.

Just when he was about to give up, Sean overheard two women talking in the food court.

"Have you been in the New Moon video shop yet? It just opened," one of them said to the other.

Sean didn't have time to be polite. "Where is it? The New Moon video shop?" he interrupted.

The woman looked surprised. "It's downstairs, right below us," she answered.

Sean shouted his thanks over his shoulder, and rushed to the nearest staircase. Then he saw it. Just ahead was the video shop. A big crescent moon filled the store's window.

Sean pushed through the doors and entered the video store. A quick look around the store told him Rita wasn't in plain sight, but he was sure there was a clue somewhere. Racks of rental videos were lined up along the wall. "Think, Sean," he told himself. "Where would Rita hide a clue?"

Frantically, Sean searched through the videos beginning with the letter M. There were a few movies with the word moon in the title, but no clue.

"What about crescent moon?" he wondered. Sean looked under C. One tape's title caught his eye: *Crescent Moon Quarry*. Sean pulled it off the rack. Sure enough, there was a photo of Rita pasted on the cover!

Sean grabbed the tape and ran to the counter. A VCR was playing an action

movie on TVs all over the store.

"Can you please do me a favor and play this on your machine for a second? It's important," Sean begged a clerk behind the counter.

The woman shrugged. "Sure," she said. "We're supposed to preview tapes

if a customer asks."

The clerk put *Crescent Moon Quarry* in the VCR. Within seconds, the picture of a crescent moon appeared on twenty different television sets.

The moon faded out, and suddenly Rita was on the screen. She was standing in front of East City High.

Rita smiled that mean smile that Sean was quickly growing to hate. "Better hurry up before the final bell rings, Sean," Rita laughed.

Then the video picture faded into blackness.

Chapter · 5

"Thanks," Sean told the puzzled clerk as he left the store. He had to get to East City High fast. But something made him stop in his tracks.

Two men were standing outside the video store. One was pointing to a TV screen in the window and talking excitedly. The other man looked angry.

There was something familiar about that angry face. It was the man Sean had seen driving the blue car that cut him off outside the cemetery!

Something strange was going on here. Sean could feel it. The men began to walk quickly back to the parking garage.

Sean followed behind them.

He had no trouble keeping them in sight. The man Sean had recognized was in his forties, of medium height, with a thick scar on his chin. His companion looked younger and was much taller, at least six feet five, Sean guessed.

The men took the stairs to the parking garage and walked out one level below where Sean had parked.

The two men argued the whole time Sean was tailing them. Sean couldn't figure out what was going on. Was this one more part of the game Rita was playing? It was strange, though. They didn't look like any friends of Rita's.

"It can't hurt to hear what they're saying," Sean thought. He crouched down and followed along after the men, making sure he was hidden behind the cars.

The men arrived at the blue car, but they paused before getting in. One of the men fumbled for the car keys. Sean was only about three feet away from them now. He could clearly hear every word the two men were saying.

"I couldn't help it! I swore that girl we were following was Rita Davenport," the man with the scar was saying.

"You're an idiot!" the tall man said. "We were so close! She was only a few steps ahead of us when we got to the mall. And you start tailing the manager from Taco Hut instead!"

"I couldn't help it. They looked exactly

alike," the scar-faced man said.

The tall man was fuming. "You screwed up from the beginning," he said. "It's your fault we lost her when she left the house tonight. We should have grabbed her hours ago."

"It's not my fault," the other man argued. "That girl is slippery. Besides, if I hadn't suggested we stop at that gas station near the cemetery, we never would have picked up her trail again."

"All I know is that you let a million bucks slip through our fingers," the tall man said. "Buzz Davenport would do anything for his little girl."

Sean gasped. These guys sure weren't friends of Rita's. If what he was hearing was true, they were planning to kidnap her tonight!

The tall man continued talking. "Anyway, I think we've still got a chance. She and that punk kid are playing some kind of game. If my guess is right, she's headed for the high school. That place will be deserted."

"What about the boy?"

"He's still bumbling around the mall. If he shows up and tries to stop us, we'll take care of him." Sean crouched down lower.

Suddenly, there was a clatter. Sean looked down. His pellet box had slipped out of his pocket and fallen to the ground. Red paint was oozing everywhere.

Sean held his breath.

"Hey, did you hear something?" Scarface asked.

"Oh, great, now you're hearing things, too," the tall man said. He unlocked the car door. "I'm not going to let you mess this up again. Let's go."

Sean stayed motionless until the car doors slammed and the blue car screeched away.

Breaking into a run, Sean headed for his car. He had to get to the high school fast. Rita's life depended on it!

Chapter · 6

On the short ride to the high school, Sean thought over his options. The kidnappers were at an advantage. They had a few minutes lead on him. There were two of them. They were probably armed.

Sean figured there was only one hope. The men knew about the game, but they didn't know Rita's moon code. It might take them awhile to search the halls of East City High, but Sean had a feeling he knew exactly where Rita was.

Both Rita's car and the kidnappers' car were in the parking lot. "That's a good sign," Sean thought. They probably hadn't found her yet.

Sean flew out of his car.

The school's front door was padlocked, but he saw a stream of light coming from the right side of the school. The door to the side entrance was cracked open.

"There's one other advantage I have, " Sean thought. "The kidnappers think I'm still back at the mall." He slipped through the open door as quietly as he could.

Fortunately, the kidnappers weren't being as careful. Instead, they were trying to flush Rita out into the open like dogs on a bird hunt.

"Come on out, Davenport!" Scarface was yelling. "There's no way you can escape!"

"One more advantage," Sean thought. "They're not too bright." To begin with, they weren't even close to where Rita was probably hiding.

But Sean knew. She had to be in the science lab in the west wing.

The astronomy club had just finished making a 3-D display of the moon's surface. Sean was sure Rita was there, waiting for him.

The only trouble was, the staircase

leading to the west wing was across the hall. There was no way Sean could cross the hall without being seen by the two men.

"Think, Sean." Suddenly, he had an idea, something he had seen in a movie once. He pulled out his flashlight. Taking a deep breath, he threw the flashlight into the hallway next to the staircase.

"Hey, someone's in that hallway!" the tall man said. The pair took off running down the hall, and Sean was able to cross to the staircase unseen.

Sean ran as fast as he could up the stairs and down the darkened hallway to the west wing. There was no time to be quiet now. He burst through the science lab door.

Sean felt something tug on his foot, and he was flung to the floor with a jerk. His foot was caught in a noose, the kind of trap people set for rabbits. But this time, he was the rabbit.

The bright lab room lights flicked on, and Sean squinted to see Rita looking down at him. She was holding a coil of rope. Before he could protest, she began to tie his hands together.

"Sorry about this, Sean," said Rita. "I never intended to trap you like this. But it serves you right for getting those two guys to help you. You're not playing by the Quarry Society rules."

Of course! Rita blamed Sean for using the two men, just as he had blamed her.

"Rita, it's not what you think! Those guys are kidnappers!" Sean protested. "I overheard them in the mall. They're going to try to get a million dollar ransom from your dad!"

Rita put her hands on her hips. "Too bad we don't give extra points for creativity, Sean. Then you might win. But we don't, so it looks like you lose big time."

Sean struggled to loosen the knots binding his hands. "I'm not kidding! I didn't come here to tag you. Check it out. I don't even have my paint pellets."

Rita looked suspicious, but she checked. A shocked look crossed her face. "You're serious, aren't you?"

"Yes! Now let's get out of here," Sean pleaded.

Both of them jumped as the

kidnappers' voices cut through the air. They were in the west wing.

Sean tried to sit up. "Run, Rita! There's no time to untie me. You can get away."

"No way," Rita said. "I got you into this. I'm not about to leave without you. We'll have to hide."

Rita quickly untied the knot around Sean's ankles, which was fairly loose. They ran behind a lab table in the back of the room.

"The lights!" Sean said. But it was too late. The kidnappers were at the door.

"Looks like somebody's doing some extra schoolwork," the tall man said. "You'd better come out, Miss Davenport. We wouldn't want to have to come in after you."

Sean's blood ran cold as he heard the sound of a pistol being cocked.

"Come out, come out, wherever you are," Scarface said.

His voice came from a few feet away.
Rita grabbed Sean's arm and pulled him
quietly toward the other side of
the room.

"Where are you?" Scarface called.
Sean breathed easier. Scarface's voice
was further away now.

"I think your little game is over."

Sean looked up. The tall man was
looking over the lab table. He and

Scarface had split up. Rita and Sean were caught.

"Rita, maybe we should just cooperate with them," Sean whispered.

"I don't cooperate with thugs," Rita said. Springing up, she grabbed a Bunsen burner from the lab table, flicked the gas jet on, and held the flame

high above her head. The tall man reached for his gun, but before he could react the sprinkler system began drenching the room with water. The sound of the fire alarm was deafening.

"Let's get out of here!" shouted the tall man. The two crooks headed out the door. "Should we go after them?" Sean yelled to Rita over the alarm.

Rita smiled. "I don't think they'll get very far."

She was right. The school fire alarm had helped bring a quick response to the scene.

A police car had seen the blue car speeding from the mall parking lot, and suspected something was up. They were cruising near the school parking lot, just when the alarm went off. The police turned into the lot—just as the kidnappers ran out of the building.

By the time Sean and Rita reached the school doors, the kidnappers had been handcuffed by the police.

Rita turned to Sean. They were both dripping wet from the sprinklers.

"Um, thanks for saving my life," she said shyly.

"I guess I should thank you, too. You could have left me there," Sean said.

"No, I couldn't have," Rita said. She looked at Sean. "You know, I've been thinking about this tie thing. I didn't mean to make such a big deal about it. Let's just call it even, okay?"

"I don't know," Sean said. "I was thinking maybe we could get together again next week."

Rita looked shocked. "You mean, another game of Quarry?"

"Well, I was thinking more like a movie," Sean said, grinning.

Rita smiled. "Sounds great . . . but on one condition."

"What's that?" Sean asked.

"Let's not go to an action movie!"